Jacob's
Music

KATIE THOMAS

Illustrated by
Chiara Carapellese

This is Jacob. Jacob is an ordinary boy who lives in an ordinary house in an ordinary village. Jacob is deaf.

Jacob can't hear the singsong of the ice cream van as it drives along his lane every afternoon after school. Jacob can't hear the cheers of footballers playing on the nearby playing fields. And Jacob can't hear the cows mooing in the field at the end of his garden. There are a lot of cows in the field at the end of his garden.

But not being able to hear is also a good thing. Jacob can't hear his mum telling him to go to bed. Jacob can't hear the words that Andy and his mean gang shout at him. And Jacob can't hear loud, scary noises.

So he can't hear the builders making a
racket next door. Or the banging of
saucepans when it's his dad's turn to make
the tea. Or the crash of thunderstorms like
his little dog, Betty, can. Sometimes Jacob
feels sad for Betty that she isn't deaf too!

Jacob also goes to an ordinary school in his village. It can be hard not being able to hear everything that is happening, but his teacher is very good at speaking clearly and always makes sure he can see her face. This means he can lip-read and understand what she says without hearing.

And some of his friends have learned signing especially for him. This is like a special language for deaf people and it's how Jacob speaks with his mum and dad and sister at home. Well, his mum and his dad anyway. His sister mostly shouts at him! Not because he's deaf. Just because that's what big sisters do.

It's a Monday morning and nearly the end of the summer term. Jacob's teacher is standing in front of the class with a big smile on her face.

"We're going to put on an end-of-term music concert," she says, "and you will all be taking part."

Jacob feels his heart do a flip and a flop. He may not be able to hear music, but he loves it just the same. Sometimes his teacher lets him sit in on orchestra practice and he can feel a beating through his feet all the way up to his head. And sometimes, if his dad's not around to look after him, his mum takes him to her choir practice. She's a soprano. That's someone who sings very high notes. Jacob can't hear her, but he can feel the vibrations coming from her mouth, like electricity zinging and crackling through space.

Jacob's teacher takes him to one side.

"Don't worry, Jacob. You will be in the concert too. I have a very special role for you."

Jacob smiles. He knows exactly which instrument he wants to play, but he waits patiently for his teacher to tell him more. He knows it's rude to interrupt.

"I will be playing the piano," she tells him. "You will stand beside me and turn the pages of my music for me. It's a very important job."

Jacob frowns.
That is not part
of his plan at all!

"I don't want to turn pages," Jacob signs when he gets home. "I want to play a proper instrument. I want to play the violin!"

"How about the tambourine? That might be possible," signs Jacob's dad.

"Or the triangle?" signs his mum. "We can speak to your teacher about it."

"Don't be silly!" says his sister. "You're deaf. Deaf people can't play the violin."

His sister doesn't bother to sign, but Jacob understands anyway. Or rather he doesn't understand. Why can't he play the violin just because he's deaf? The violin is his favourite instrument to watch when he sits in on orchestra practice. He loves the way the bow moves backwards and forwards. He loves the way the violinist's arm sweeps gracefully from side to side. He loves the way her fingertips skip nimbly from string to string. To Jacob, it's like signing, and he knows all about signing.

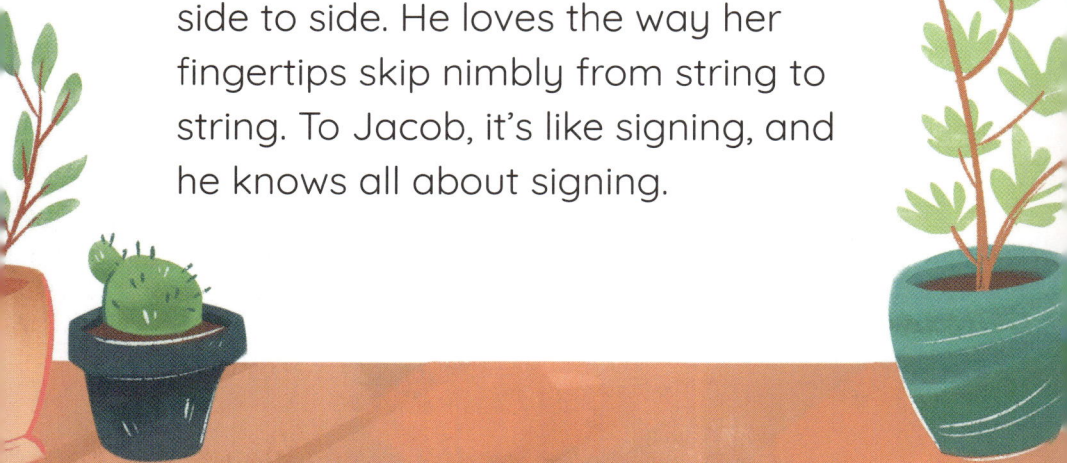

The next day, Jacob comes home with a violin.

"You may borrow it, Jacob," his teacher had said. "But you can't play it in the concert. It takes a long time to learn how to play the violin, and the concert is in just two weeks."

Jacob thinks it can't be that hard. First of all, he has a go playing to his dad.

"I'm trying to finish off some work, Jacob," signs his dad. "Maybe go and play to your mum."

"I've actually got a bit of a headache, Jacob," signs his mum. "Perhaps some other time when I'm feeling better."

"Jacob, that's the most awful noise I've ever heard!" shouts his sister. "Go and play somewhere else. Somewhere far away. Like the bottom of the garden!"

Even Betty doesn't seem to like his music!

It's a nice, warm evening, so Jacob wanders down to the end of the garden where he knows no one will be able to hear him. He sits down on the grass and starts to play. Maybe his music doesn't sound good to other people, but for Jacob, the humming under his chin, the woosh under his arm and the tingling in his fingers is the best feeling in the world.

As Jacob plays, a curious cow wanders down and peers at him over the fence. Then another. And then another. Before long, the whole herd of cows is there. Standing still. Watching him. Listening to him. They hardly move. Just the odd twitch of an ear or the swish of a tail.

When it's time for bed,
Jacob stands up and
bows to the cows. He thinks
one of them almost bows
back before they all turn
and wander off.

Jacob goes to the end of the garden every evening and plays. And every evening the cows turn up, one by one, and watch him and listen to him. Quietly. Silently.

When it's time to give back the violin, Jacob is very sad. Playing to the cows made him happy, but now he can't do it anymore. His teacher needs the violin for the concert. And violins are too expensive to buy, even if he saved up his pocket money for years and years. Jacob knows this because he's worked it out, and he's very good at sums.

The day of the concert comes, and Jacob stands by the piano ready to turn the pages of the music when his teacher nods her head. All the rest of his class have been given instruments.

"You can play the tambourine or the triangle if you want," his teacher had said the day before. But Jacob had shaken his head sadly. If he couldn't play the violin, then he didn't want to play at all.

The school hall is very crowded.
Everyone has come to watch.
Jacob can see his mum and dad
sitting in the front row. His sister
is at the back with her friends.

Jacob does a good job. He knows that because his teacher smiles every time he turns the page at the right time. But it isn't the same. He hasn't got a violin. He isn't making music.

As the last note is played, everyone stands up to clap. And everyone in the orchestra stands up to bow. Jacob bows too. Even though he doesn't feel that he's done anything to deserve being clapped.

CLAP

CLAP

CLAP

"And now we have
a very special visitor,"
says Jacob's teacher.

Jacob looks up and sees a tall man walking towards him. Jacob feels his heart racing and his legs go wobbly. He knows this man. He knows him very well. This man is the farmer who owns the cows in the field at the end of the garden. And the fact that he is here, at the concert, walking straight towards Jacob, can only mean one thing. He must have found out about Jacob playing to his cows and he must be angry. And now everyone is going to know. Everyone is going to know that deaf people can't play the violin, not even to cows!

"Hello, Jacob," says the farmer. And then the farmer turns to face everyone in the hall. Everyone has gone quiet. Everyone is looking at the farmer and at Jacob.

"Jacob has been
playing the violin to my cows,"
says the farmer. "I haven't heard
what he plays, but I can see him
playing from my farmhouse."

Jacob is now sure that he is in big,
big trouble. But the farmer is still
speaking and he is smiling.

"My cows LOVE Jacob's music," says the farmer. "I know this because they have not been producing enough milk recently, but since Jacob has been playing to them, they have been producing milk like never before."

"Jacob," says the farmer, "I want you to keep playing to my cows and I hope this will help you to do that."

From behind his back, the farmer offers a parcel to Jacob. A violin-shaped parcel. Jacob's teacher is smiling now too.

"We WILL teach you to play it, Jacob," she says, quietly.

And now everyone is clapping. And Jacob feels proud for the first time. So proud.

Did you know…?

1   There are estimated to be over 300 different sign languages currently in use around the world. The two most well-known are American Sign Language (ASL) and British Sign Language (BSL).

2   BSL is the fourth most used language in the UK. On 28th June, 2022, BSL was recognised in law as an official language of Great Britain. It now has the same importance as other languages such as English, Welsh, Irish and Scottish Gaelic.

3   As well as signs, BSL uses facial expressions, gestures and body language to communicate. Sign language has its own system of grammar, and many deaf people have their own unique 'name sign', which is like a nickname.

4   *The Smurfs* was the first animated show to have a character use sign language. *Smurfing In Sign Language* is the episode that introduced the deaf wood elf, Laconia.

5   A child of a deaf adult is given a special term in the deaf community. They are called Child of Deaf Adult (CODA). In the 2021 film *Coda*, Ruby Ross, the only hearing person in her family, is torn between helping her family's struggling fishing business and fulfilling her dream as a singer.

6   Deaf singer-songwriter Mandy Harvey appeared on Season 12 of *America's Got Talent*. She sang an original song while playing the ukulele. It was her dad who had asked her to start playing the guitar with him. "I didn't want to at first," said Mandy, "but I said yes because he's my dad and I love him. I was watching the chord changes and doing those with him. And then eventually he asked me to learn a song to sing, which I thought was ridiculous!" But she accepted the challenge and earned a 'Golden Buzzer' from Simon Cowell.

7   In 2021, deaf actress Rose Ayling-Ellis won BBC's *Strictly Come Dancing* show with her partner, Giovanni Pernice. "I'm not relying on the music," she said. "I'm relying on counting and the beat."

8   Ludwig van Beethoven, the great classical composer, was almost totally deaf by the time he was 44 years old. So how did he continue composing without his hearing? The explanation given is that music is a language with rules. Knowing the rules of how music is made enabled him to compose a piece of music without hearing it.

9   Music really does help milk production in cows. Some farmers have installed high-priced music systems in their barns to keep their cows soothed and relaxed. Beethoven's *Pastoral Symphony* and Simon & Garfunkel's *Bridge Over Troubled Water* have proved to be big hits in the milking shed.

10   A few years ago, more than 1,000 entries were received in a song contest that allowed people to create their own mash-up. The winner was chosen by the cows themselves, based on the amount of milk produced while the songs were played.

To find out more about signing, visit
www.british-sign.co.uk

WACKY BEE

Published by
Wacky Bee Books
Shakespeare House,
168 Lavender Hill,
London,
SW11 5TG,
UK

ISBN: 978-1-913292-55-3

First published in the UK, 2022

© 2022 Katie Thomas and Chiara Carapellese

Design by David Rose

Picture credits:
Pixabay.com / ArtTower / Gordon Johnson
iStock.com / Fizkes

Printed by AkcentMEDIA

www.wackybeebooks.com